Animal Alphabet Coloring Book

by Nina Barbaresi

DOVER PUBLICATIONS, INC., New York

Note

Animals come in all shapes and sizes—and all colors and letters, too, as you'll learn when you color the pages of this book. Every letter of the alphabet is here, accompanied by its own menagerie of creatures whose names begin with it. Try to identify all the animals, and check your guesses with the identifications printed upside-down at the bottom of the page. From the domestic Dog and Cat to the exotic Quagga and Zebu: they're all here for you to meet and color!

Published in Canada by General Publishing Company, Ltd., 30 Lesmill Road, Don Mills, Toronto, Ontario.

Published in the United Kingdom by Constable and Company, Ltd., 3 The Lanchesters, 162–164 Fulham Palace Road, London W6 9ER.

Animal Alphabet Coloring Book is a new work, first published by Dover Publications, Inc., in 1991.

International Standard Book Number: 0-486-26698-2

Manufactured in the United States of America
Dover Publications, Inc., 31 East 2nd Street, Mineola, N.Y. 11501

1: Armadillo. 2: Anteater. 3: Alligator. 4: Aardvark. 5: Antelope. 6: Ant.

1

1: Bear.　　2: Bull.　　3: Bat.　　4: Beaver.　　5: Bison.　　6: Butterfly.

1: Crab.   2: Chipmunk.   3: Crocodile.   4: Chicken.   5: Cow.   6: Cat.

3

1: Dolphin   2: Donkey   3: Duck.   4: Dinosaur.   5: Deer.   6: Dog.

1: Fawn. 2: Fish. 3: Fox. 4: Flamingo. 5: Ferret. 6: Frog.

1: Goose.   2: Grasshopper.   3: Giraffe.   4: Goat.   5: Gorilla.   6: Gerbil.

1: Hippopotamus. 2: Hare. 3: Hen. 4: Horse. 5: Hawk.

1: Iguana.   2: Ibex.   3: Ibis.   4: Impalas.

1: Jerboa.   2: Jaguar.   3: Jay.   4: Jackrabbit.   5: Jackal.   6: Jellyfish.

10

1: Koala.   2: Kitten.   3: Kinkajou.   4: Kiwi.   5: Kangaroos.

1: Lobster. **2:** Leopard. **3:** Lizard. **4:** Lamb. **5:** Lion. **6:** Llama.

12

1: Mouse.   2: Musk-ox.   3: Mole.   4: Moose.   5: Mule.   6: Monkey.

1: Narwhal.　2: Nutria.　3: Newt.　4: Newfoundland dog.　5: Nautilus.

1

2

6

3

5

4

1: Octopus.   2: Otter.   3: Owl.   4: Orangutan.   5: Ostrich.   6: Opossum.

15

1: Porcupine.   2: Penguin.   3: Peacock.   4: Panda.   5: Pig.   6: Parrot.

16

1: Quetzal.   2: Quagga.   3: Quail.

1: Raccoon. 2: Rhinoceros. 3: Robin. 4: Rooster. 5: Reindeer. 6: Rabbit.

18

1: Skunk.　2: Swan.　3: Seal.　4: Squirrel.　5: Snail.　6: Snake.

1: Tiger.   2: Toucan.   3: Turtle.   4: Tapir.   5: Toad.   6: Turkey.

1: Uakari.   2: Urubu.   3: Unicorn.

1: Vulture.   2: Vampire bat.   3: Vervet monkey.   4: Vicuna.   5: Viper.

1: Woodchuck.　2: Walrus.　3: Whale.　4: Weasel.　5: Wolf.　6: Woodpecker.

23

1: Xiphias.   2: X-ray of a horse.